D1180793

BANANA BOOKS

A series of bright, funny, brilliantly imaginative stories written by some of today's top writers especially for newly fluent readers. All of the books are beautifully illustrated throughout with full-colour pictures. Choose from the new titles below or from the list on the inside back cover.

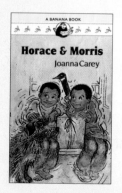

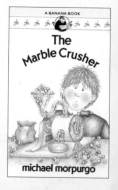

The Marble Crusher

Illustrated by
FRANCES THATCHER

HEINEMANN · LONDON

To Pieter, Meryl,

Maxine and Matthew

William Heinemann Ltd
Michelin House
81 Fulham Road
London SW3 6RB

LONDON · MELBOURNE · AUCKLAND

First published 1992
Text © Michael Morpurgo 1992
Illustrations © Frances Thatcher 1992
ISBN 0 434 97670 9

Produced by Mandarin
Printed in Hong Kong

A school pack of BANANA BOOKS 49-54 is
available from Heinemann Educational Books
ISBN 0 435 00108 6

Chapter One

ALBERT WAS TEN years old. He was a quiet, gentle sort of a boy with a thatch of stiff hair that he twiddled when he was nervous.

He had moved to town from the countryside. 'We have to go where the work is,' his mother had told him, and there was work in the town.

So Albert came from his little village school to a new school, a school which was noisy and full of strange faces. The other children called him Bert, or Herbert,

neither of which was his name. They kept asking him questions and they wouldn't leave him alone.

There was somewhere to get away from it all, behind the bike shed in the playground, but never for long. By the end of each day Albert felt like a sponge squeezed dry. He smiled so much that it hurt. He tried to laugh at everyone's jokes, and he believed everything they told him. He was naturally a trusting

child, and now, in the first weeks
of his new school, he wanted to
please everyone, to make friends.

They teased Albert of course, and he
was easy enough to tease, but Albert just
smiled through it all. They called him
"Twiddler!" and Albert smiled and went
on twiddling his hair. He did not seem to
mind.

It was Sid Creedy who discovered that
Albert would believe almost anything he
told him. They were playing football in
the playground in break when Sid turned
to his friends and said, 'Watch this.' He
dribbled the ball over towards Albert, and
his friends followed him.

'My Dad,' said Sid, 'he played centre-
forward for Liverpool. Did for years.
Then they asked him to play for England,
but he didn't want to – he didn't like the
colour of the shirt.'

Chapter Two

THAT EVENING ALBERT told his mother all about Sid Creedy's father, but his mother wasn't listening, she was too busy washing up.

Encouraged by his success, Sid Creedy's stories became more and more fantastic. 'You know Mr Cooper, Bert?'

'You mean the P E master?'

'Yes, that's him.' Sid spoke in a confidential whisper, his arm around Albert's shoulder. 'Well Bert, no one else knows this, but Mr Cooper isn't really a teacher at all – he's an escaped monk.'

'How do you know that, Sid?' said Albert.

'You look at his head,' said Sid. 'It's all bald in the middle isn't it? You know, like Friar Tuck. Anyway I found his brown cloak in the boot of his car. He always wears sandals, and he never swears. And haven't you noticed he sings louder than anyone else in Assembly?'

'But why did he escape?' said Albert.

Sid shrugged his shoulders. 'Didn't like the food,' he said.

'And he knows you know?'

'Course he does, but I told him I'd keep it quiet. You're the only one I've ever told, Bert.'

Albert went home and told his mother, but his mother was busy making his tea.

'Mum,' he said, 'that Mr Cooper at school, he's an escaped monk.'

'Yes dear,' she said. 'Now get those wet shoes off before you catch your death.'

Chapter Three

BACK AT SCHOOL Sid Creedy told Albert more and more of his secrets. Every teacher at school it seemed had a deep, dark secret – even the Headmaster, Mr Manners.

'He's got six wives,' said Sid one day, 'like Henry the Eighth.'

'He hasn't!' said Albert.

'Oh yes he has,' said Sid. 'And that Mrs Manners that teaches the Infants, she's just one out of the six. And he's got twenty-two children.'

'He hasn't!' said Albert.

'Oh yes he has,' said Sid, 'and there's two more on the way.'

Back in the classroom, as Sid told his

friends, he was triumphant. Albert had
swallowed it hook, line and sinker.

At home, Albert tried to tell his

mother about Mr Manners. 'Honest, Mum, he's got six wives,' he said with his mouth full of toast.

'What's that dear?'

'Mr Manners, Mum. He's got twenty-two children as well,' said Albert, 'like Henry the Eighth. And he was away from school today.'

'Well, I hope it gets better,' said his mother. And that was that.

Chapter Four

CONKERS WERE OVER and it was the marble season in mid-November. Now Mr Manners hated marbles.

'Treacherous things, marbles,' he said in Assembly one morning. 'Slip on one and you can break a leg, just like that. In the playground, yes, play with them all you wish, but inside my school there will be no marbles. If I see, or so much as smell a marble inside my school, it will be confiscated. And you know what that means.'

'What does it mean, Sid?' Albert asked after Assembly.

'What does what mean?'

'Con . . . confiscated. What does it mean?'

Sid smiled inside himself. 'Crushed,' he said. 'Crushed, that's what it means.'

'Crushed?'

'Same every year,' said Sid, and he

turned to his friends. 'Isn't that right, lads?' And they all nodded and turned away to hide their smiles.

Sid went on in a hushed voice. 'It's like this, Bert. If your marbles are confiscated by old Manners, that means he takes them away and puts them through his machine – a marble crusher.'

'A marble crusher?'

'A marble crusher. He keeps it in his room under his desk. I've seen it. We've all seen it. And that's where they all go.'

Chapter Five

BACK AT HOME Albert had his own
collection of marbles, but they were no
ordinary marbles. They were silver ball-
bearings. He had seventy-five of them
now, pea size to conker size. They were all
lined up on the mantelpiece above his bed.
Everyone at school had glass marbles but
no one else had silver ball-bearings.
Albert was very proud of them.

Over half-term Albert polished them
till they shone, and the day school began
again he took six of the big ones with him
into school. They were cold and heavy in
his pocket. And what a sensation they
created!

Albert was very good at marbles, and
he knew he was particularly good with his
silver ones. Over rough ground they kept
to a truer line than the glass ones that
often bounced off course. So by
lunchtime he had won ten marbles. One

of them was a blood red, a lovely deep red marble, highly prized because there was a white mist gliding around inside it. Of course everyone wanted to play Albert to try and win one of his silver marbles, but Albert chose the rough ground and he outplayed them all.

It was in reading time, after lunch, that Sid Creedy challenged him to play marbles, but *inside* the classroom. Albert didn't really want to. He preferred the long distances and the potholes of the playground. But he did not want to upset his friend and so he agreed. In the excitement of the game he quite forgot Mr Manners' rule about playing marbles inside the school.

Even on the smooth floor in amongst the chair legs Albert went on winning. He was crouching under the teacher's table, taking careful aim, when Mr Manners came in behind him silently.

'Albert,' he said. 'Albert, are you playing marbles?'

'Oh . . . yes sir,' and Albert remembered at once – he remembered the punishment too and he began to twiddle his hair.

'They will all have to go, all of them mind,' said Mr Manners. 'Empty your pockets, lad,' and he held out his big chalky hand. 'I'm surprised at you, Albert, and disappointed – very disappointed.'

Albert took them out of his pocket one by one and dropped them into Mr Manners' hand. His winnings went first – the blood red too – and then last of all his six great heavy silver ball-bearings. It was as if his blood was being taken from him. The fist closed before his eyes and his marbles were gone.

'A pity, Albert,' Mr Manners said, shaking his head. 'A terrible pity. Lovely marbles too. But you were warned. And

we cannot have people breaking school rules can we now?'

'No sir,' said Albert, wondering how long it would be before his marbles went through the crusher, how much longer they had to live.

'Hard luck,' said Sid, when Mr Manners had gone out. 'You can only just hear the machine, Bert,' he went on. 'It's all modern and silent.'

'You mean the marble crusher?' said Albert, blinking back his tears.

Sid nodded. 'I'm afraid so. They're gonners, Bert. Ten minutes and they'll be so much dust. It's Japanese, very efficient.'

Chapter Six

ALBERT WENT HOME that afternoon miserable. He could not bear to think of his beautiful silver marbles being ground down to dust. He was crying bitter tears by the time he reached his front door. He

cried up against his mother's apron, and in between the heaving and the snivelling his mother heard the whole story of Mr Manners' terrible machine, how it was unfair, how he would never see his six silver marbles again, nor the blood red, how he hated Mr Manners, all the teachers and everyone at the school, including the dinner ladies.

This time Albert's mother had to listen. She was inside the school gates within five minutes, still in her apron, dragging Albert along by his hand. Albert did not want to go. He did not want her to make a fuss. He did not want to be hauled red-eyed and snivelling through the school gates. Albert's mother never even knocked on the staffroom door. She burst into the room, her eyes searching out the Headmaster.

Mr Manners was half way to his mouth with a cup of tea, and the other teachers sat around him not knowing quite where to look.

'Mr Manners,' she stormed, 'I sent my son to your school because I thought you would look after him and care for him. And what happens? Albert tells me you have taken away his collection of marbles and you have destroyed them with some horrible machine – Albert calls it ''a marble crusher'' or some such thing.

Never in all my days have I heard of such
cruel goings on inside a school. I'm telling
you, the authorities are going to hear
about this. You haven't heard the last of
this, Mr Manners. If this is how teachers
treat children these days . . . ' And so on
and so on.

Mr Manners had put down his teacup

and was holding up his hand, much in the same way a policeman might try and stop traffic. 'I think there has been some misunderstanding,' he said. 'Certainly I confiscated Albert's marbles . . . '

'Confiscated! Confiscated! You crushed them Mr Manners, not confiscated them.'

Mr Manners frowned. 'Did Albert tell you that?' And Mr Manners looked down at Albert. Albert was completely bewildered. Never had he seen his mother this angry. He twiddled his hair furiously until his mother slapped his hand away.

'That's what Albert told me,' she said, 'and my son's no liar, Mr Manners. He wouldn't invent such things, he's not like that.'

'Oh, I know that,' said Mr Manners, and he turned to Albert. 'Now tell me,

Albert, who told you about this machine, this marble crusher?'

'It was Sid, sir,' said Albert, 'Sid Creedy. He said you've got a great big marble crusher under your desk. He said all the marbles you take away are crushed down to dust. Japanese he said, and very efficient.'

Mr Manners was nodding and he was smiling too. 'And what else does he say, Albert?'

Slowly, very slowly, the truth was beginning to dawn. Albert was beginning to understand. The teachers around were all smiling. He knew Sid Creedy had been lying to him and he wanted his own back.

'He said you've got six wives, sir, like Henry the Eighth, sir; and you've got

twenty-two children and there's two more on the way. And he said that Mr Cooper's an escaped monk.'

'Mr Cooper,' said Mr Manners, 'tell me, are you an escaped monk?'

Mr Cooper smiled down at Albert and ruffled his hair. 'No,' he said. 'I've never

been a monk, and the way I feel about
Sidney Creedy just now I don't think I'd
ever qualify. But Mr Manners, what
about you? We've only ever met one of
your wives and two of your twenty-two
children. Where do you keep the others?'

So the whole web of lies was unravelled
in front of him. Albert saw his mother

laughing with them and he felt ashamed
of himself and his stupidity. But Mr
Manners put a comforting arm around
him.

'Never you mind, Albert,' he said. 'It
seems to me you have a nice trusting
nature, and it also seems to me that I shall
have to teach Master Sidney Creedy a
little lesson.'

Chapter Seven

NEXT MORNING, AFTER Assembly, Mr Manners made them all sit down in the School Hall. He had something to say, something very important he said. He put his hands on his hips and cleared his throat.

'Teachers can be wrong, children,' he began, 'like anyone else they can be wrong from time to time. And I was wrong to confiscate Albert's marbles yesterday. You see, in the heat of the moment I quite forgot that it takes two to play marbles, doesn't it? Now I can't remember, so I'm going to have to ask whoever was playing marbles with Albert

yesterday to stand up.'

Albert looked down at the floor and twiddled his hair. Everyone else looked at Sid Creedy so he had to stand up.

'Sid Creedy,' said Mr Manners nodding slowly. 'Well, Sid, it seems only

fair then that I also confiscate your marbles. I think that's only right, don't you?' Sid said nothing. 'You'd better come up here, Sid,' said Mr Manners; and reluctantly Sid poured a bagful of marbles into Mr Manners' hand.

'Nice ones,' said Mr Manners examining them closely. 'What a pity, what a terrible pity.' And then he went out. Sid Creedy came back and sat down next to Albert.

'Will he put them in the marble crusher?' Albert whispered.

'Don't be silly, Bert.' Sid Creedy was irritated. 'Course not, you dumb Herbert, there's no such thing as a marble crusher. I was having you on wasn't I? You'd believe anything wouldn't you?'

From down the corridor came a distant electrical hum like a muffled power drill. It lasted for a few seconds and then there was a long silence. They heard the staffroom door slam and then Mr Manners' crisp footsteps coming back towards the School Hall.

'There,' he said as he shut the door behind him. 'That's that then.' He was holding two paper bags. One he gave to

Albert and one to Sid Creedy. 'They've been through the marble crusher,' he said. 'Just like sand now, colourful sand.'

And he spoke now to the whole school. 'Well children,' he said. 'You can see now that you would be well advised *never* to play marbles inside my school again. If you do it will merely mean more work for my marble crusher. It's Japanese you know. Very efficient!'

A BANANA BOOK